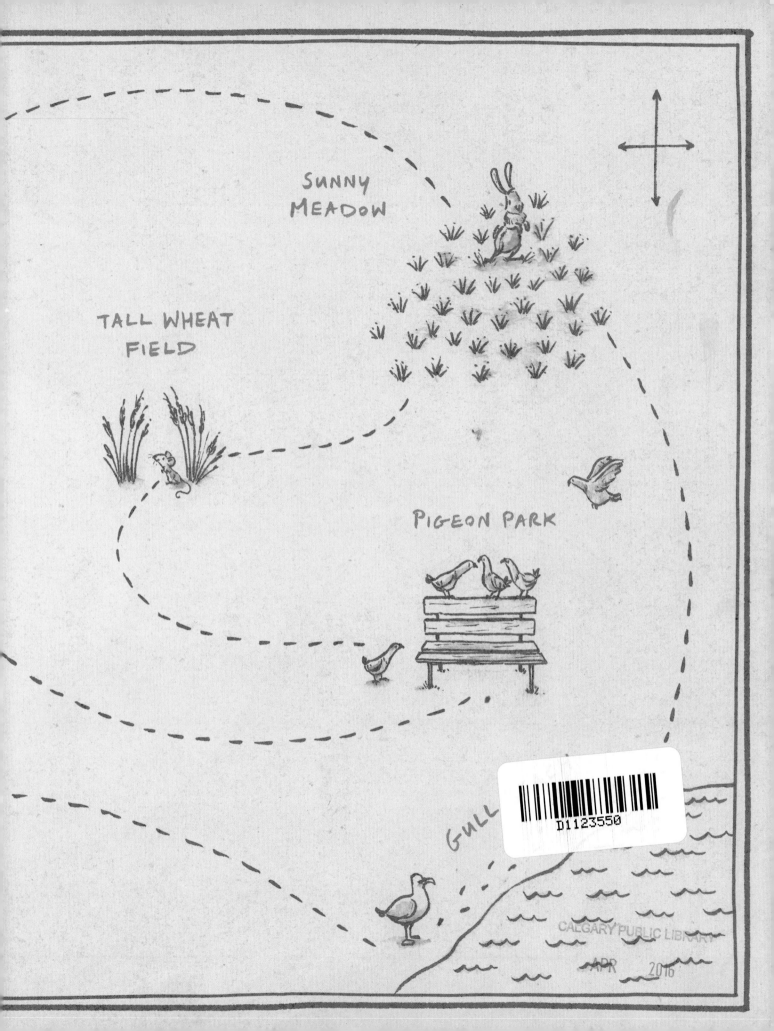

SUNNY
MEADOW

TALL WHEAT
FIELD

PIGEON PARK

GULL

This belongs to :

For Mum and Dad xx

little bee books

An imprint of Bonnier Publishing Group

853 Broadway, New York, New York 10003

Copyright © 2016 by Ciara Flood

First published in Great Britain by Templar Publishing.

This little bee books edition, 2016.

LITTLE BEE BOOKS is a trademark of Bonnier Publishing Group, and

associated colophon is a trademark of Bonnier Publishing Group.

Manufactured in China 0081215

First Edition 2 4 6 8 10 9 7 5 3 1

Library of Congress Cataloging-in-Publication Data is available upon

request.

ISBN 978-1-4998-0192-7

littlebeebooks.com

bonnierpublishing.com

the
PERFECT
PICNIC

Ciara Flood

little bee books

OAK LODGE

Squirrel and Mole were the best of friends.

They did everything together.
They danced together,

they baked cakes together,

they went on bike rides together,

and they especially liked
to paint pictures together.

One day Squirrel and Mole decided to have
a picnic. Squirrel wanted it to be the most
perfect picnic ever.

"No butter on the sandwiches!" said Squirrel.
"Right you are, Squirrel," said Mole
(even though he loved butter
on his sandwiches).

After much preparing, everything
was ready to go into the picnic bag . . .

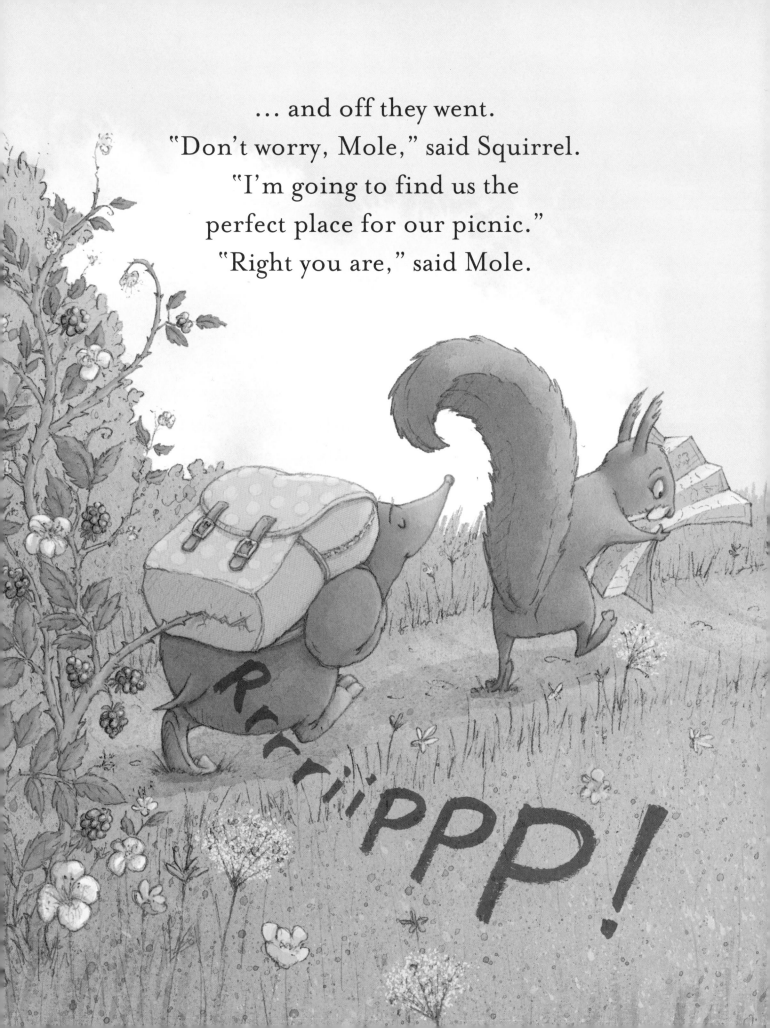

... and off they went.
"Don't worry, Mole," said Squirrel.
"I'm going to find us the
perfect place for our picnic."
"Right you are," said Mole.

RrriiiPPPP!

"This is a very pretty meadow," said Mole.
"Yes, but it's not perfect," said Squirrel.
"We need more shade."
"Right you are," said Mole.

"This field has shade," said Mole.
"Yes, but there's too
much of it," said Squirrel.
"Right you are," said Mole.

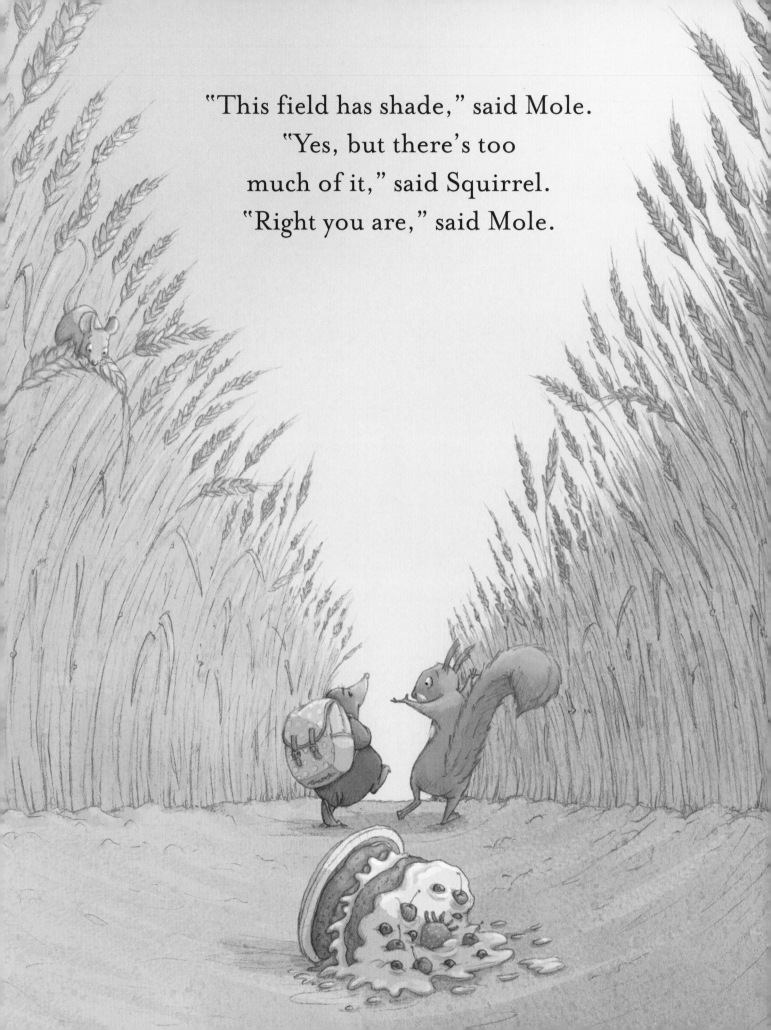

"Well, how about here?" asked Mole.

"It's far too busy," said Squirrel.
"Right you are," said Mole.

"There's nobody else up here," said Mole.
"Yes, but it's much too windy," said Squirrel.
"Right you are," sighed Mole.

The two friends went
to a lot of places . . .

. . . a river,

"Too wet. . . ."

a cave,

"Too dark. . . ."

a beach . . .

"Too sandy. . . ."

. . . until Squirrel finally stopped.

"I've found it, Mole!" she said.
"The perfect place to have our picnic!"

"But Squirrel, we've already been here!" groaned Mole.

Just then, Mole noticed something else.
"Uh-oh!" he said.

OOOOO!"

wailed Squirrel.

"This is the worst picnic ever!"

"Ahem!" said a small voice.

"I believe this is your cake?" said Mouse.

"And these are your apples," said Otter.

"I found your rug," said Bat.

"I have your sandwiches," said Seagull.

"And we have your crackers," said the Pigeons.

"Here are your plates," said Goat.

"And is anyone looking for a nice cup of tea?" asked Hare.

The apples were bruised, the cake
was squished, the plates were chipped,
the forks and spoons were bent, the rug was dusty,
the sandwiches were sandy, the tea was cold,
and the crackers were very much eaten.

"Don't worry, Squirrel," said Mole.
"We can fix this."

It was not the perfect picnic that
Squirrel had planned,

but it was a lot of fun!

"I'm already looking forward to our next picnic,"
said Squirrel.

"Me too," said Mole. "But next time,
let's have butter on the sandwiches."

"Right you are, Mole," said Squirrel.
"Right you are."

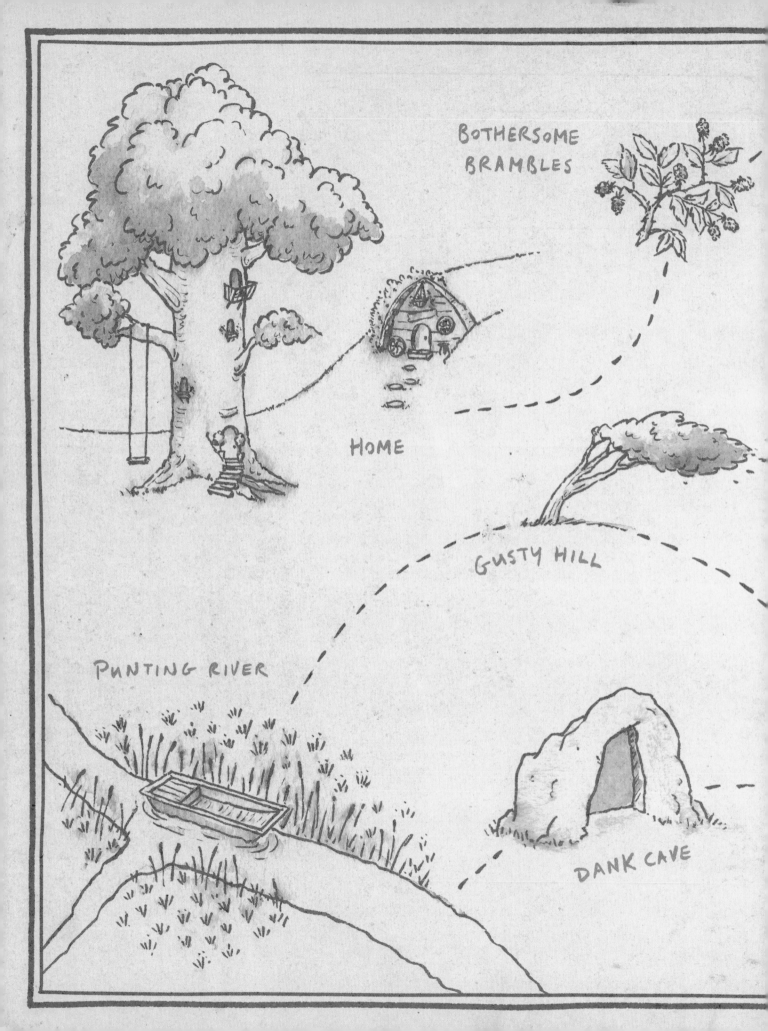

BOTHERSOME
BRAMBLES

HOME

GUSTY HILL

PUNTING RIVER

DANK CAVE